My Big Brother, Boris

Liz Pichon

This book is dedicated to my Mark

Scholastic Children's Books
Commonwealth House, 1-19 New Oxford Street
London WC1A 1NU, UK
a division of Scholastic Ltd
London ~ New York ~ Toronto ~ Sydney ~ Auckland
Mexico City ~ New Delhi ~ Hong Kong

First published in hardback in the UK by Scholastic Ltd, 2004
First published in paperback in the UK by Scholastic Ltd, 2004

Copyright © Liz Pichon, 2004

ISBN 0 439 97368 6

This is me, Little Croc, and this is my family,
Mum Croc, Dad Croc and my big brother, Boris.
We all live happily in a lovely part
of the swamp.

Boris is a bit older than I am, but we still have lots of fun together. Sometimes we go swimming . . .

. . . and sometimes Boris lets me play in his room.

Our favourite game is 'Guess What I Am?'
Mum and Dad join in, but they are RUBBISH!

Boris always wins because he is the best.

It's TOO LOUD!

But lately Boris has been spending more and more time
with friends his own age. They all go to his room
and listen to really loud music for hours.
"TURN THAT NOISE DOWN!" shouts Dad when he's
had enough. I knock at the door. "Can I come in too?" I ask.
But nobody hears me.

Tomorrow we are having a big party for Boris
because it's his birthday. I CAN'T WAIT!
I am making a special party game for us to play.
All his friends start laughing.
"We're too old to play silly party games," they tell me.
"But Boris likes party games!" I say.
"NO I DON'T!" Boris snaps at me.
Which is not very nice, and a
bit odd because Boris and I
play games all the time.

Pin the tail on the DONKEY

When Boris isn't with his friends he looks a bit sad.
"Let's go swimming," I say to cheer him up.
"We could play 'Guess What I Am?'" I add hopefully.
"I told you . . . I'm far too old to play silly games,"
Boris says, in a really HORRID, grumpy voice.

Go away...

I don't think Boris
likes me any more.

"Boris won't play with me," I tell Mum.
"All he does these days is . . .

EAT ...

SLEEP ...

... and hang out with his friends. Boris is just no fun any more." Mum sees that I am very upset.

So she gives me a BIG cuddle, which makes me feel much better. And we start to blow up all the balloons for the party.

The party is about to start! I am really excited, but
Boris isn't even up yet. And when he does come out
of his room, we all get a big SHOCK.

Boris is wearing
a snout ring!
Mum and Dad go
BONKERS!

They have a HUGE row, and Boris storms off back to his room.
"What about the party?" I ask.
"I don't want a stupid party now!" he shouts crossly.

I LIKE IT!
IT'S MY SNOUT!

Now I'm REALLY upset.
I go next door to see
Granny and Grandpa
Croc.

"Oh dear, looks like everyone needs cheering up,"
says Granny Croc.
"I've got a good idea," Grandpa says to me.
So we go back to the party together.

Boris is still sulking when all his friends arrive.
"We're so sorry," Mum and Dad tell them. "Boris won't
come out of his room."
"But we've brought presents for him!" they say.

"And we've got a special party game," I add in a very
LOUD voice.
"What a shame," says Granny Croc. "Boris will just
have to miss it."
Very slowly the door begins to open . . .

She looks familiar...

. . . and this time it's Boris who gets a big shock!

"Can anyone guess who these lovely young crocs are?"
asks Grandpa Croc.

Everyone has a good look at the old photos.

No one seems to know, but I think I do . . .

"IT'S YOU, MUM AND DAD!" I shout . . .
and I win the game.

Boris says it's the best party EVER
and all his friends agree.
Everyone sings Happy Birthday . . .

. . . and I give him his cake.

Boris even plays the party game I made.

I think I'm really lucky to have a big brother like Boris.

He's the best big brother in the whole world . . .

Babies

KT-430-389

For Tim

Designed by Louise Millar

Printed and bound in Belgium by Proost
for the publishers Piccadilly Press Ltd.,
5 Castle Road, London NW1 8PR

ISBN: 1 85340 679 1 paperback
1 85340 684 8 hardback

3 5 7 9 10 8 6 4 2

Typeset in 20pt Stone Serif

A catalogue record for this book is available from the British Library

ALSO AVAILABLE IN THIS SERIES:

BABY LEMUR
ISBN: 1 85340 541 8 (p/b)

BABY TIGER
ISBN: 1 85340 504 3 (p/b)

BABY ELEPHANT
ISBN: 1 85340 641 4 (p/b)

*Susan Hellard is an acclaimed illustrator who lives in North London.
She has been published by many publishers, and is well-known
for bringing to life the character Dilly The Dinosaur.*

Baby Panda

SUSAN HELLARD

Piccadilly Press • London

Pu Lin and his mother lived together in a beautiful bamboo grove in the mountains of China.

When Pu Lin was a baby his mother carried him everywhere. She never put him down for more than a minute.

Pu Lin's mother found lots of crunchy
bamboo shoots for him to eat.
He grew bigger every day.

Pu Lin's mother was very proud of him.
"Now you are big enough to walk on your own
and to climb trees!" she said one day.

But naughty Pu Lin was rude to his mother. "Walking is boring," he declared crossly. "And I don't want to climb trees. Bamboo shoots are boring, too! I'm tired of them." He threw himself down and pounded the ground with his paws.

"You are a sulky boy!" said his mother.
"I'll leave you on your own for a while
to think things over."
And she padded away to chew bamboo shoots
on the edge of the grove.

Pu Lin stomped off to the pool to have a drink. He lapped up the water till his tummy felt like a tight little drum.

Then he toppled over into the bushes.
"Everything is so boring," he groaned.

Suddenly, his mother sniffed the air. She smelled danger. There were jackals nearby!

Silently and swiftly she ran back to Pu Lin.
"Hurry! We must climb up a tree to safety!"
she whispered. But Pu Lin was so full of water
that he could hardly move.

His mother grabbed him by the scruff of the neck and ran with him to the foot of a big tree.

"I can't carry you. You must climb
up yourself!" she panted.

"I can't! I can't!"
whimpered Pu Lin.
Then he looked round
and saw the jackals' eyes.

Pu Lin was so frightened!
Digging his claws into the tree trunk
he started to climb.

Higher and higher he and his mother
climbed – right to the very top of the tree,
far away from the jaws of the jackals.

Sitting at the top of the tree,
Pu Lin saw the most beautiful view.
Huge pine trees,
a great winding river,
distant snowy mountains,
and endless bamboo groves.
This wasn't boring. This was exciting!

Then Pu Lin found himself a little perch
where he could reach the highest,
juiciest bits of bamboo.
They tasted wonderful – not boring at all.

Pu Lin's mother called
to him. "The jackals
have gone. I can carry
you down now."
"It's boring being carried,"
said Pu Lin.
"I can climb down myself.
It's much more fun!
Come on, I'll race you!"
"That's my boy!" laughed
his mother.

Facts About Pandas

Pandas are found only in remote mountain areas of South West China.

Pandas have a gentle disposition and a slow, clumsy movement. Mature pandas are large and heavy. They have cat-like claws which make them agile tree-climbers, but they are awkward on the ground.

Pandas are almost exclusively vegetarian, with strong teeth for chewing fibrous vegetation – mainly bamboo. They spend all day eating.

Pandas seldom stray from the dense bamboo groves and clear mountain streams and rivers, although in summer they may move up the mountain to a higher altitude.

Pandas enjoy drinking almost as much as eating and are often reluctant to leave the river. They may drink so much their bellies become bloated and they can hardly move, making them flop down like drunkards.

Pandas do not hibernate or store food. They live alone and have no regular den, sleeping anywhere that takes their fancy, in clumps of bamboo or hollow trees.

Pandas may be attacked by a number of predators, including wolves, jackals, leopards or brown bears. They escape by climbing trees.

Females give birth after five months, usually to between one and three cubs. Only one receives its mother's personal care and the others rarely survive.

A baby panda weighs about 100 grams and is 13 to 15 centimetres long. It's born with closed eyes and has soft white down which develops grey then black patches over a few weeks.

Pandas can live for 25 years. They are very playful, especially after meals.